REAL
mvpkids

Counting Critters

Sophia Day®

Written by Megan Johnson   Illustrated by Stephanie Strouse

The Sophia Day® Creative Team-
Megan Johnson, Stephanie Strouse, Marla Conn,
Kayla Pearson, Timothy Zowada, Mel Sauder

A **special thank you** to our team of reviewers who graciously
give us feedback, edits and help ensure that our products
remain accurate, applicable and genuinely diverse.

Published and Distributed by MVP Kids Media, LLC -
Mesa, Arizona, USA
Printed by Prosperous Printing Inc. -
Shenzhen, China

Designed by Stephanie Strouse

ISBN 978-164370760-0
DOM Aug 2019,
Job # 11-001-02

May your childhood be filled with adventure, your days with hope and your learnings with wisdom, and may you continuously grow as an MVP Kid, preparing to lead a responsible, meaningful life.

– SOPHIA DAY

Grab your notebook, bug box, hat.

Let's explore some habitats!

How many critters live in our yard?

Where can we find them? Let's look hard.

What is
a habitat?

Up high in webs and hives they're found,

down in the grass or underground.

We'll study critters face to face,

and leave them right back in their place.

Where do critters live?

Busy working 'round the hive,

How many bumble bees?

I see five!

Three on red flowers, two on blue,

making five with three plus two.

One finds shade, four in the sun,

making five with four plus one.

$$3 + 2 = 5$$

$$4 + 1 = 5$$

Crawling on the grassy floor,

how many ladybugs?

I see four!

Two that crawled and two that flew,

making four with two plus two.

Three in the grass, and one on me,

making four with one plus three.

$$2 + 2 = 4$$

$$1 + 3 = 4$$

Jumping, hopping, brown and green-

how many grasshoppers?

I see three!

Two that chirp, one on the run,

making three with two plus one.

2 + 1 = 3

Creeping, spinning, crawling through-

how many spiders?

I see two!

One spider spinning; one's web is done,

making two with one plus one.

Wiggle, squiggle, sure looks fun!

How many worms?

I see one!

Just one worm, no more around

unless you look....

1 + 0 = 1

...under the ground!

Now how many do you see?

Count back up to five with me!

One... two... three... four... five!

Flying, hopping, spinning, wiggling,

creeping, crawling, jumping, squiggling.

Underground, on trees, in hives,

we counted critters. Give me five!

What words from the story describe the way critters move?

meet our

featured in
Counting Critters™

Blake James

Annie James

Gabby Gonzalez

Lucas Miller

LeBron Miller

HELPFUL TEACHING TIPS
Head. Heart. Hand.

Informing Minds

Number sense refers to a person's broad understanding of numbers and fluency in math skills. In this book your child will be exposed to the following components of number sense:

- Understanding parts of a whole (3+1=4; 2+2=4)
- Naming numbers
- Counting with one-to-one correspondence
- Reading mathematic equations

Number sense encourages students to think flexibly about problem solving and teaches that numbers are meaningful with sensible and consistent outcomes. Developing number sense at an early age is an indicator for future success in math.

Research supports that curiosity leads to success in math. Allow your child to spend time outdoors in environments that encourage exploration. Find topics your child is interested in and provide opportunities to link those interests to math.

Moving Hearts

A child's attitude toward education begins very young and depends on whether learning is made to be exciting. Teach counting by using their favorite toys. Model an excitement for learning by showing joy while working with your child.

Help children develop a love for nature by taking time to slow down and look closely. Activities that develop focus and attention to detail in nature are calming and contribute to long-term academic success. Keep simple items like a magnifying glass, pencils and notebooks handy and model observation skills. Focus on the process rather than the outcome to help your child gain the most from these experiences.

Before taking your child out to look at bugs, make sure you're aware of bugs in your area that are unsafe. Start teaching your child the difference between friendly bugs and harmful bugs, especially if you live in an area with stinging or venomous insects.

Help children see math all around them! Point out when your young child is using math, such as comparing the size of their cookie with another or counting rocks they collect in their pockets. This will help develop number sense and make math exciting.

As you read through this book, point at the colored number sight words on each page as you say it. The more you read the book, the more familiar your child will become with these sight words. Their confidence will soar after a few repetitions when they can "read" the word for themselves and associate the written word with the correct number.

Support organization skills and set recognition by providing plenty of opportunities to sort objects by size, color and shape. Use beans, cereal, blocks or other toys of various sizes, colors and shapes. Sorting activities strengthen number sense and help prepare your child for organizing their own toys or putting away the silverware!

Try this activity to help your child understand parts of a whole: Choose three small objects that you can easily hold in your hands. They should all be the same, such as three beans, three pompom balls or three paperclips. Show your child the objects with your palms open and count them together. Next, quickly hide one object in a closed fist while keeping the other two visible. Have the child count the object left in your palm, then ask your child how many are hidden in your fist. Next, try hiding two of the objects in your fist. When your child is able to do this easily with three objects, slowly increase the total number of objects.

Directing Hands

For additional tip and reference information, visit www.mvpkids.com.

Grow up with our MVPkids

CELEBRATE!™
Board Books
Ages 0-6

Our **CELEBRATE!™** board books for toddlers and preschoolers focus on social, emotional, educational and physical needs. Helpful Teaching Tips are included in each book to equip parents to guide their children deeper into the subject of each book.

MIGHTY TOKENS
READ TOGETHER
Ages 4-8

Our **Mighty Tokens™** paperback books for Pre-K to Grade 3 help emerging readers experience positive concepts with their parents. Children will learn valuable reading skills as their parents read one side of the page and the child is encouraged to read the other side.

help me BECOME
Early Elementary
Ages 4-10

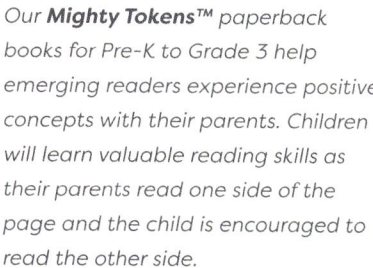

Our **Help Me Become™** series for early elementary readers tells three short stories of our MVP Kids® inspiring character growth. Each story concludes with a discussion guide to help the child process the story and apply the concepts.

help me UNDERSTAND™
Elementary
Ages 6-12

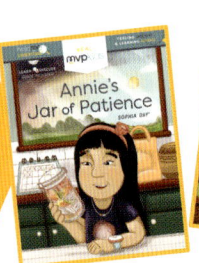
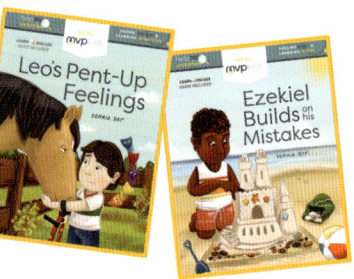

Our **Help Me Understand™** series for elementary readers shares the stories of our MVP Kids® learning to understand and manage a specific emotion. Readers will gain tools to take responsibility for their own emotions and develop healthy relationships.

Celebrate!™ Paperbacks

Ages 4-8

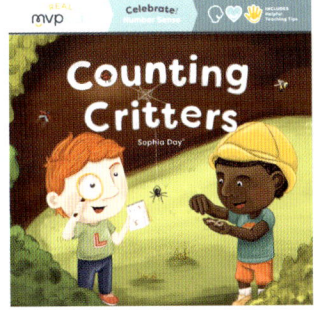

Counting Critters
Sophia Day

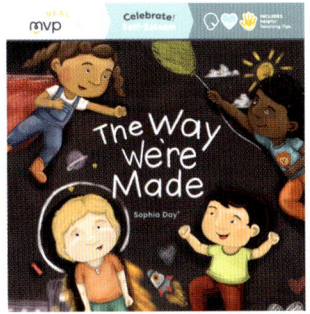

The Way We're Made
Sophia Day

My Family Loves Me
Sophia Day

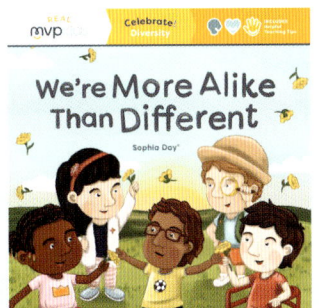

Treasured Wisdom
Sophia Day

We're More Alike Than Different
Sophia Day

Smile for the Dentist
Sophia Day

Check Up with the Doctor
Sophia Day

Our **Celebrate!™** paperback books for Pre-K to Grade 2 focus on social and emotional learning. Helpful Teaching Tips are included in each book to equip mentors and parents. Also available are expertly written curriculum and interactive e-book apps. These books are perfect for classrooms and home schooling!

Inspire Me-Books™

- Inspire Character®, Enrich Entertainment™, Nurture Literacy™, Expand Education™ and Cultivate Mentorship™ with our interactive **InspireMe-book™** apps. These apps are designed to expand the experience of our content.

- Functions include audio of Sophia Day reading the book, learn-to-read options such as slow reading with highlighted words or choosing a specific word to be pronounced along with interactive games.

www.mvpkids.com

Yong Chen

Leo Russo

Frankie Russo

Julia Rojas

Aanya Patel

Faith James

Blake James

Sarah Cohen-Goldstein